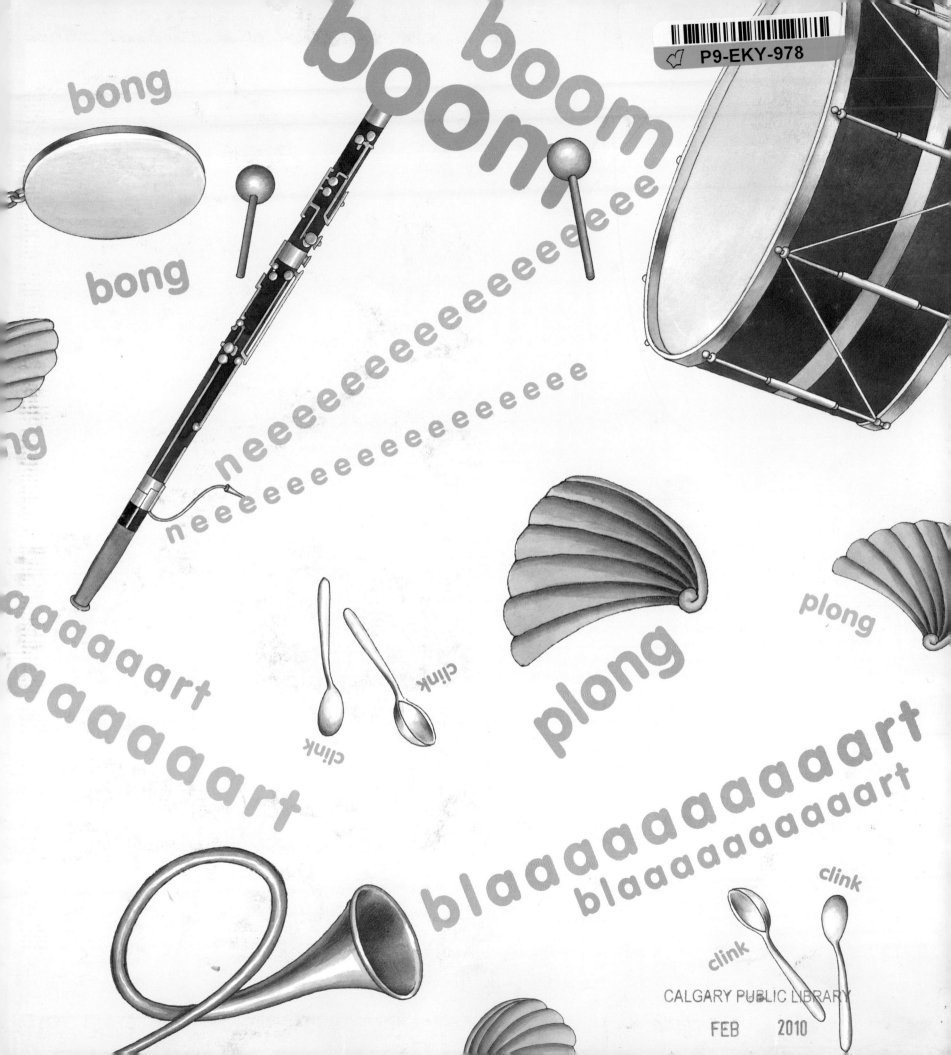

author's note

My son came home one day from a Dalcroze music class singing "the little gnome song." It was only one verse—and he sang it over and over again. For fun, he and I made up new verses and sang them together, changing them each time. We never wrote them down, but we shared the little gnome song so many times that certain verses became favorites and the song grew longer and longer—and longer! And each time, it got louder, too! This book was made in gratitude to the Dalcroze method, which encourages children to share their love of music and their gift for making music with others.

Please join in and add your own verses and sounds to ours.

—Laura Geringer

For Adam, with love
—L. G.

Atheneum Books for Young Readers
An imprint of Simon & Schuster Children's Publishing Division
1230 Avenue of the Americas, New York, New York 10020
Text copyright © 2010 by Laura Geringer
Illustrations copyright © 2010 by Bagram Ibatoulline
All rights reserved, including the right of reproduction
in whole or in part in any form.
ATHENEUM BOOKS FOR YOUNG READERS is a registered trademark of Simon & Schuster, Inc.
For information about special discounts for bulk purchases,
please contact Simon & Schuster Special Sales
at 1-866-506-1949 or business@simonandschuster.com.
The Simon & Schuster Speakers Bureau can bring authors to your live event.
For more information or to book an event, contact the Simon & Schuster Speakers Bureau
at 1-866-248-3049 or visit our website at www.simonspeakers.com.
Book design by Sonia Chaghatzbanian
The text for this book is set in Helvetica Rounded.
The illustrations for this book are rendered in
watercolor, acrylic-gouache, and ink.
Manufactured in China
First Edition
2 4 6 8 10 9 7 5 3 1
Library of Congress Cataloging-in-Publication Data
Bass, L. G. (Laura Geringer)
Boom boom go away! / Laura Geringer ; illustrated by Bagram Ibatoulline.
p. cm.
Summary: A cumulative rhyme in which a young boy emphatically and noisily
tells his parents to go away when they say it is time for bed.
ISBN 978-0-689-85093-6
[1. Stories in rhyme. 2. Bedtime—Fiction. 3. Musical instruments—Fiction.]
I. Ibatoulline, Bagram, ill. II. Title.
PZ8.3.G314Boo 2010
[E]—dc22
2009017400

BOOM BOOM GO AWAY!

laura geringer

bagram ibatoulline

Atheneum Books for Young Readers ••• New York London Toronto Sydney

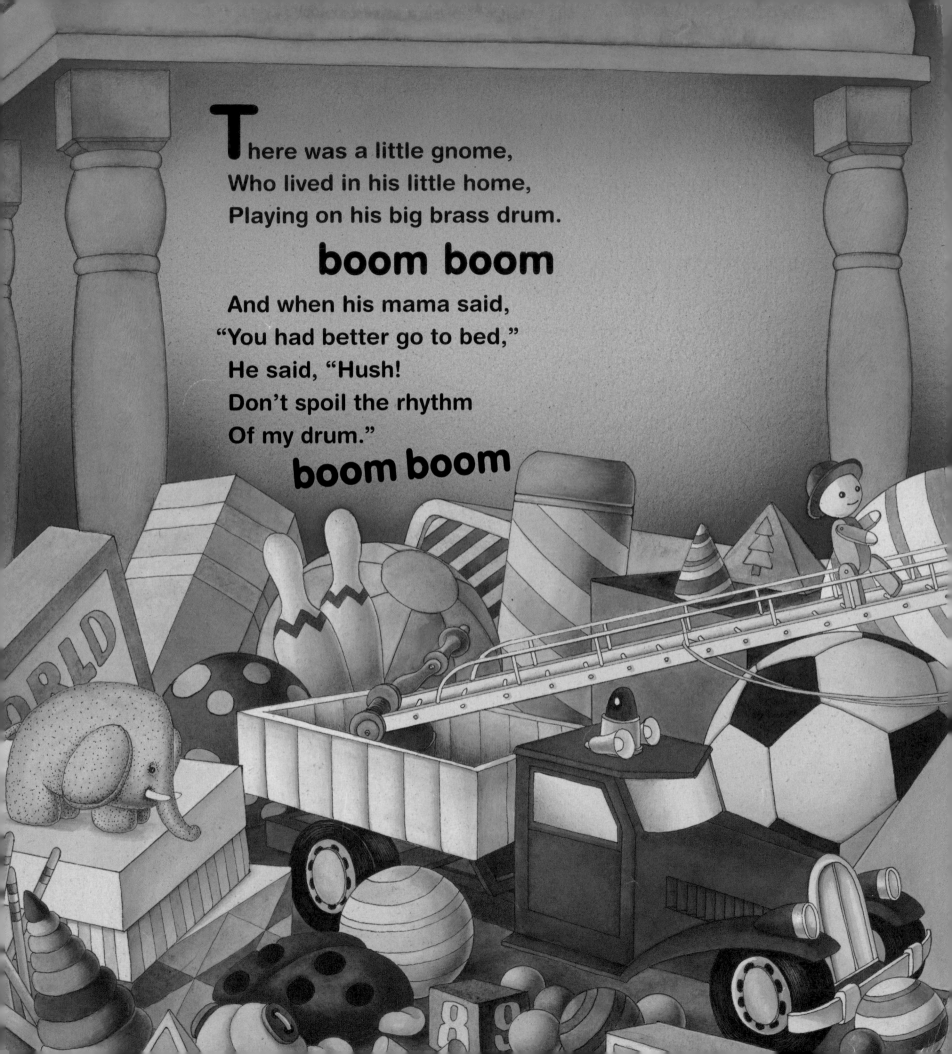

There was a little gnome,
Who lived in his little home,
Playing on his big brass drum.

boom boom

And when his mama said,
"You had better go to bed,"
He said, "Hush!
Don't spoil the rhythm
Of my drum."

boom boom

There was a little elf,
Who lived underneath the shelf,
Playing on his ancient gong.

ding ding

And when his papa said,
"You had better go to bed,"
He said, "Hush!
Don't spoil the rhythm
Of my gong."

"Go away."

ding
ding

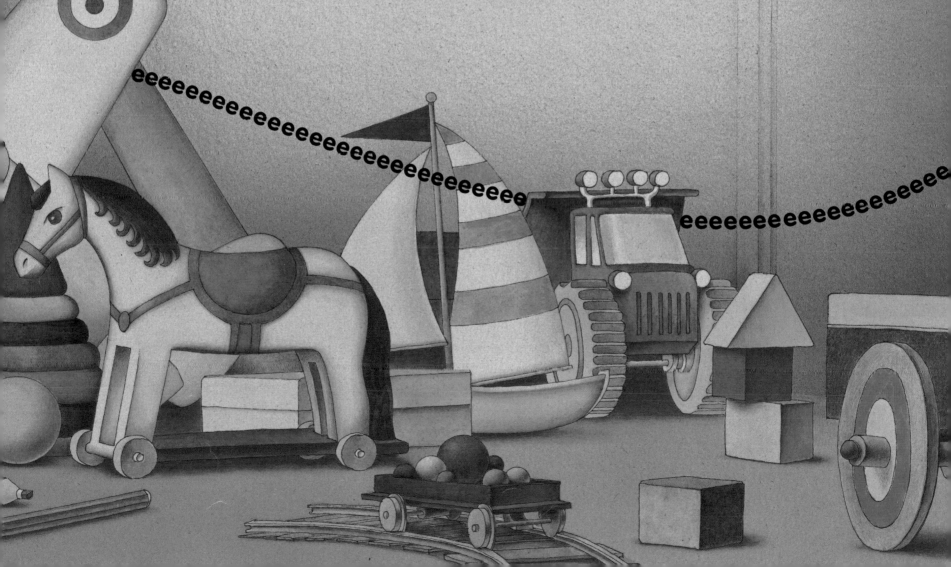

There was a little prince,
Who made everybody wince,
Playing on his big bassoon.

neeeeee neeeeee

And when his mama said,
"You had better go to bed,"
He said, "Hush!
Don't spoil the rhythm
Of my tune."

neeeeeeee

eeeeeeeeeeeeeeeeeeeeeeeeeeeeeeeee

eeeeeeeeeeeeeeeeeeeee

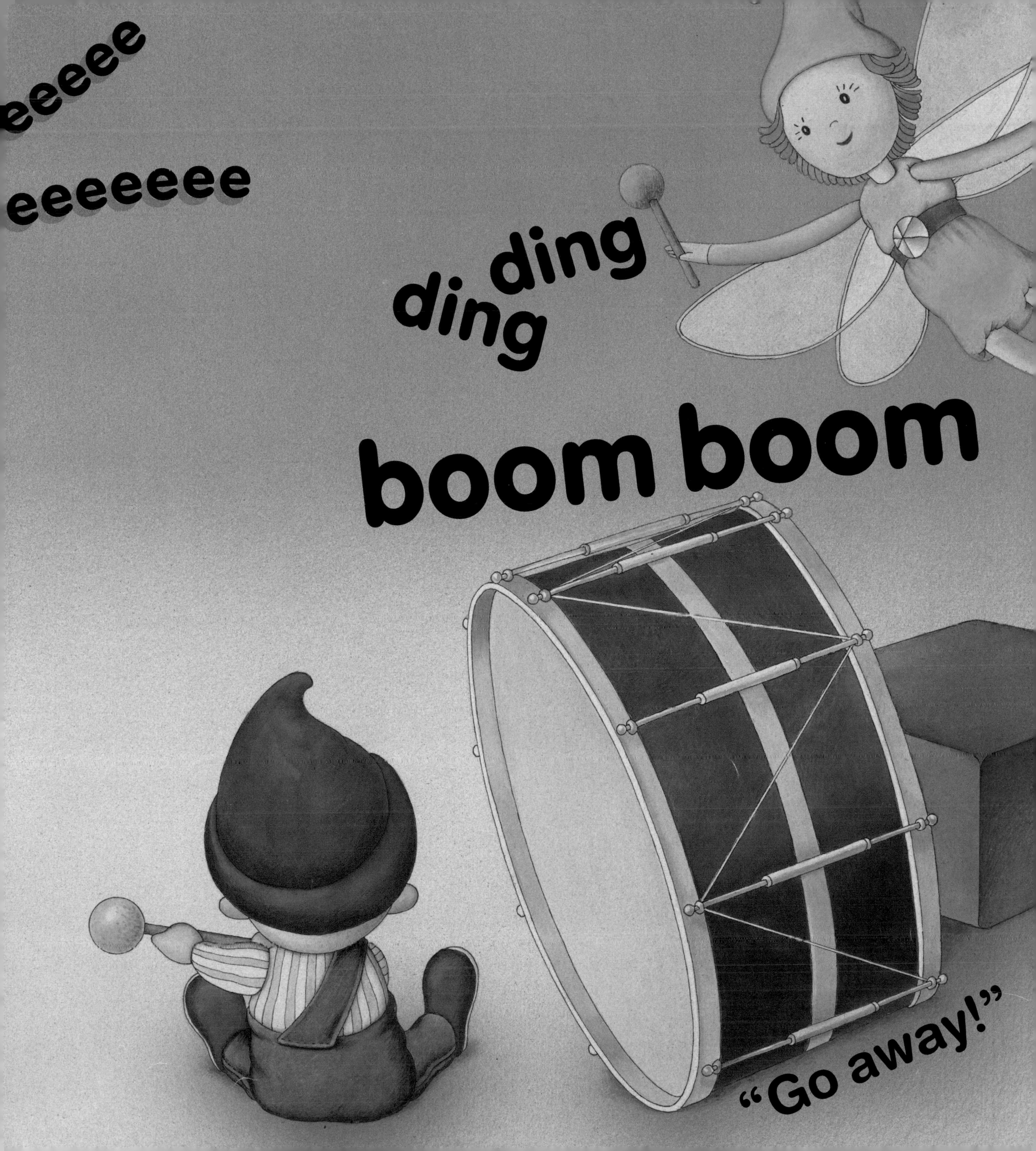
eeeee
eeeeeee
ding
ding
boom boom
"Go away!"

There was a little knight,
Who stood guard beside the light,
Playing on his battle bells.

bong bong

And when his papa said,
"You had better go to bed,"
He said, "Hush!
Don't spoil the rhythm
Of my bells."

bong
bong

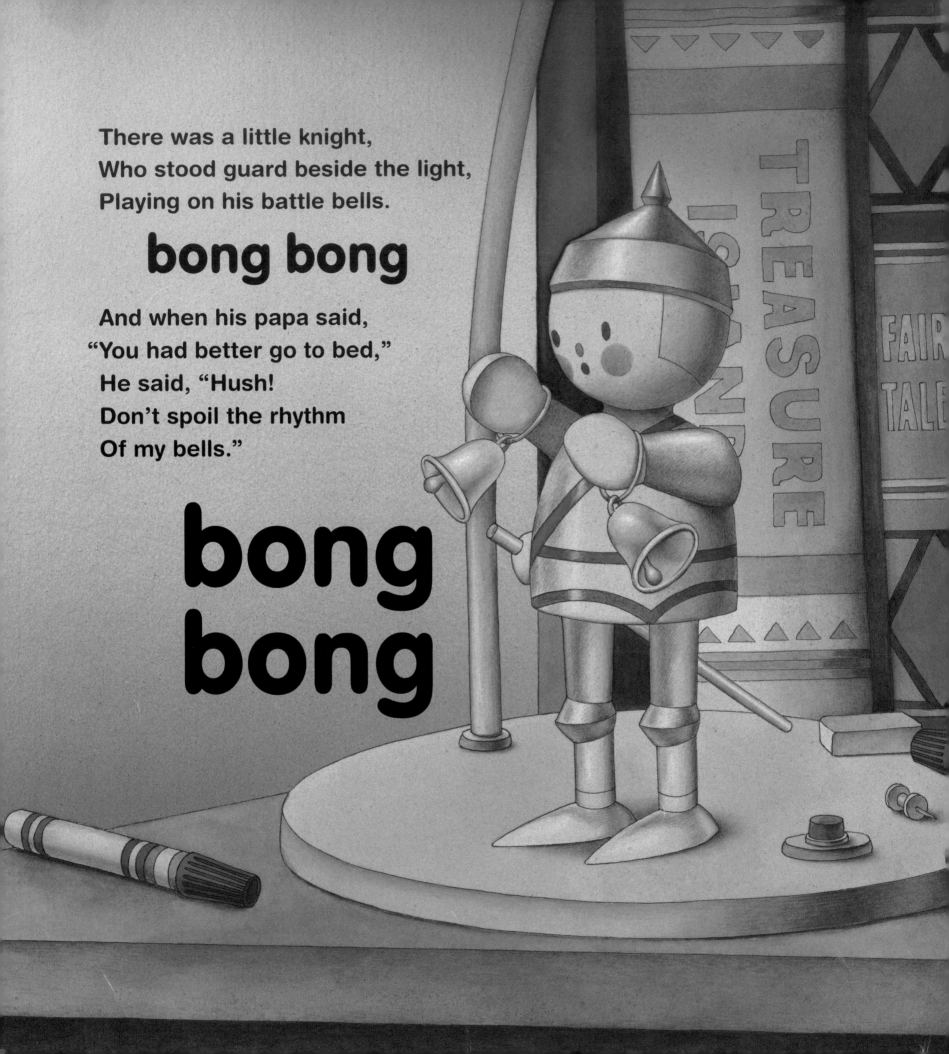

THE ADVENTURE

GLUE

There was a little bot,
Who lived in a flowerpot,
Playing on her steely spoons.
clink clink

And when her papa said,
"You had better go to bed,"
She said, "Hush!
Don't spoil the rhythm
Of my spoons."

There were three mermaid girls,
With a treasure chest of pearls,
Playing on their seashell harps.

plong plong

And when their mama said,
"You had better go to bed,"
They said, "Hush!
Don't spoil the rhythm
Of our harps."

There was a little bear,
Who made everybody stare,
Playing on his big brass horn.

blaaaaaaaart
blaaaaaaaart

And when his papa said,
"You had better go to bed,"
He said, "Hush!
Don't spoil the rhythm
Of my horn."

There was a little gnome,
Who lived in his little home,
Playing on his big brass drum.

boom boom

And when his mama said,
"You had better to go to bed,"
He said, "Hush!
Don't spoil the rhythm
Of my drum."

**boom
boom**

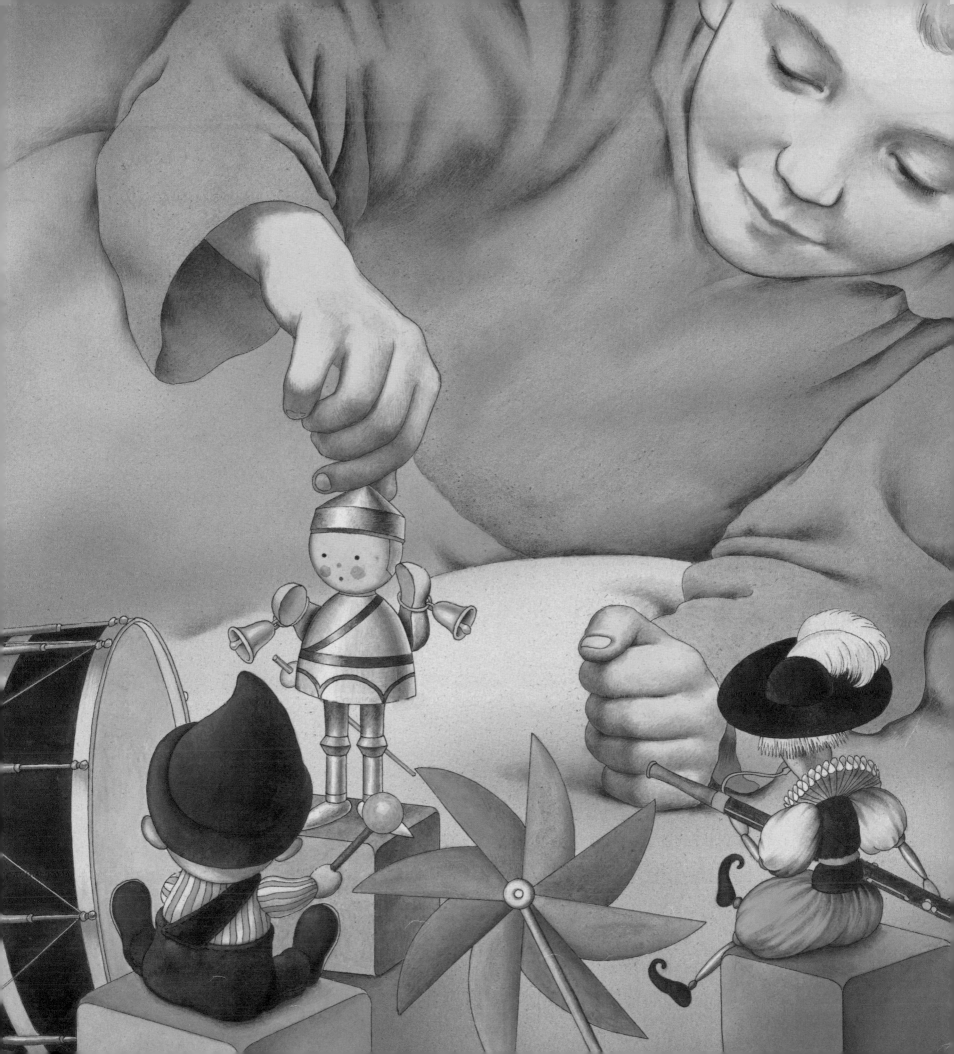

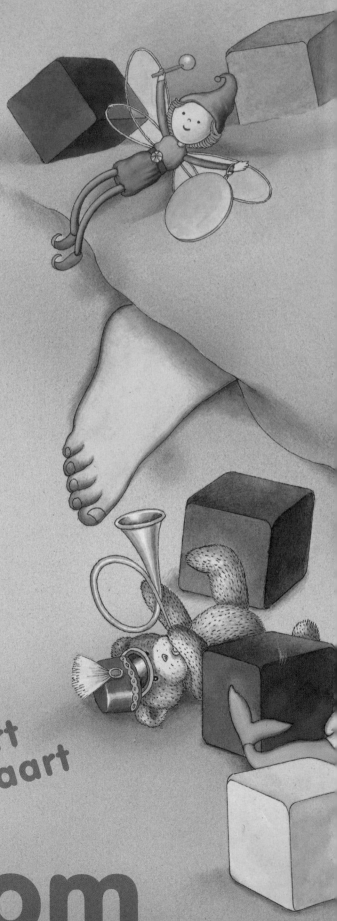

"Go away."

boom boom

ding
ding

neeeeeeeeeeeeeeeeeeeeeee
neeeeeeeeeeeeeeeeeeeeeeeee

bong
bong

clink
clink

plong
plong

blaaaaaaart
blaaaaaaart

boom boom

"GO AWAY!"

Hush, hush . . .

boom boom

"Go away."